by Bonnie Highsmith Taylor

Cover and Inside
Illustration: Christine McNamara

For Lennise "Cookie" Thomas

About the Author

Bonnie Highsmith Taylor is a native Oregonian. She loves camping in the Oregon mountains and watching birds and other wildlife. Writing is Ms. Taylor's first love. But she also enjoys going to plays and concerts, collecting antique dolls, and listening to good music.

Printed in the United States of America. For information, contact
Perfection Learning® Corporation
Phone: 1-800-831-4190
Fax: 1-712-644-2890
1000 North Second Avenue, P.O. Box 500
Logan, Iowa 51546-1099.

Paperback ISBN 0-7891-2931-0
Cover Craft® ISBN 0-7807-8961-X
Printed in the U.S.A.
6 7 8 9 10 PP 08 07 06

Contents

1

In Trouble Again!

At first I thought it was a siren going off. Right in my bedroom. Gol, was the house on fire?

Then I realized it was Mom. She was standing right over me. She was screeching bloody murder right in my ear.

"Scott! Get out of that bed! Right now!" Mom yelled, nearly breaking my eardrums.

Boy, she was mad about something!

In the back of my mind, I knew right away what it was. But I hated to admit it.

It had to be about Joker. It always was.

The whole family—Mom, Dad, and my brother—had been in an uproar ever since I'd gotten him. That had been last fall—for my twelfth birthday. What a great birthday present!

I loved that little black pony more than anything in the world. All my life I'd wanted a horse of my own. My brother had had his own horse for three years.

"We can't afford to get two horses right now," Dad had said when he bought Wayne's horse. "Maybe later. Why don't you boys share him?"

Well, in the first place, Wayne wasn't into sharing. Besides, it was his birthday present.

"Anyway," Wayne argued, "a horse isn't something you can share."

I agreed. A horse should belong to just one person.

So Mom and Dad had decided I'd have to wait. Until I was older, and they could afford it.

I'd gotten Joker nearly five months ago. And—well—things hadn't been going very well. That's really putting it mildly too. It had been total chaos!

The siren went off again—louder.

"I mean it, Scott! Get up out of that bed! Immediately!" Mom screeched.

She emphasized every word with a stomp of her foot. The bed was shaking.

"But, Mom," I groaned. I squinched my eyes closed as tight as I could. "It's Saturday."

I scooted down in the bed and pulled the covers over my head. Mom jerked them off. "Get up!" she demanded.

I drew my knees up to my chin. "Aw, Mom!"

I was wishing I knew how to look pitiful. That had worked so well when I was five and six. But it didn't work when you were twelve. And a guy at that.

It probably worked for girls—no matter how old they were.

Oh, well. It probably wouldn't work on Mom now anyway. Not as mad as she was.

Through the window I could hear my brother. He was laughing like an idiot. He sounded like a giraffe gargling. If giraffes gargled.

Wayne is three years older than I am. He thinks that that makes him more important. He's about as important as crust on bread. And I hate crust.

Mom walked over to the window. She raised the blind and looked out.

"I'm glad your brother thinks it's funny," she said. "Because I don't."

She turned back toward me. "And neither will you," she said. "Especially when you see what your precious pony just did."

I sat up in bed. I took a deep breath to prepare myself for whatever. I dreaded looking out that window.

"Because," Mom went on, "you are going to rewash the entire laundry."

"Huh!" I gasped. I flew to the window.

Oh, no!

All of Mom's clean laundry was on the ground. Or the fence. Or blowing across the road.

Except for Mom's skimpy pink nightie. It was draped across Joker's nose.

Wayne was leading Joker back through the gate. Joker had kicked it open again. My brother was laughing. Loud! So loud he was nearly drowning out Joker's whinny.

Oh, why couldn't Mom use her clothes dryer? The way other people did.

Mom picked up my jeans and T-shirt off the floor. She threw them at me.

"Dress!" she ordered. "You have five minutes."

I made it in three.

I ran around the yard. I picked up towels, shirts, socks, and undies. They were filthy.

Wayne handed me the nightie he'd taken off Joker's nose. "Wonder if this looks as good on Mom as it looks on that stupid horse," he snickered.

I jerked it away from him. It was wet with horse slobber. I crammed it into the basket with the rest of the stuff.

"Don't forget those things," Wayne said. He pointed across the road. "The things that blew into

Mrs. Carter's yard."

I hurried over to our neighbor's yard. I hoped no one would see me. But Mrs. Carter seldom missed anything. Sure enough—her door opened, and there she was.

"What are you doing, dear?" she called from her porch.

I smiled up at her. "Just picking up my dad's undershorts," I answered.

2

What's in a Name?

It was almost noon before I finished the laundry. Mom ended up helping me.

I was putting Dad's jeans in the washer when Mom let out a howl. "No!" she screeched.

I jumped three feet. "What?" I asked.

"Don't put the jeans in with the underwear," she said.

She pulled the jeans out of the washer. She slopped water all over the floor—and me.

"Why not?" I asked.

"You just don't," she snapped.

Well, how was I supposed to know? I'd never done laundry.

Mom finished the rest of the laundry. But she made me mop up the water she'd slopped.

I had a feeling this was going to be a sad Saturday.

Dad wasn't home when Joker broke out. He was helping his friend fix his car. Dad's a mechanic. His friends are always getting him to work on their cars.

Dad didn't see the mess my pony made. But he heard about it—all through lunch. And mostly from Wayne.

"You should have seen him, Dad," Wayne said. "It was a riot! Joker scattered clothes and stuff all over. Even across the road. Your shorts ended up on Mrs. Carter's lawn!"

"Oh, great," Dad groaned.

He took a swallow of coffee. Then he turned to me. "He's not working out, Scott," Dad said. "I think we'd better find another home for him."

"But, Dad—" I began.

"I've told you before, Scott," Dad interrupted. "We can't keep an animal that acts the way Joker does."

Dad took a couple of bites of salad. Mom and Wayne went right on eating. I couldn't believe it. I couldn't swallow a bite. And they were stuffing their faces. Just as though nothing was wrong. As though Dad hadn't just said I'd have to get rid of Joker.

I'd die without Joker. I loved him so much.

Then Mom started. "Do you realize how much trouble that horse has caused?" she asked. "He's destroyed the flower bed twice. Knocked down my rose trellis. And nearly killed your father."

That set Wayne off. He really roared. He laughed so hard he urped up an olive. A whole olive. It landed in his chocolate pudding. The smart mouth.

Joker's incident with Dad was something I wanted to forget. But of course, I couldn't. It hadn't really been Joker's fault though. At least I didn't think so.

I had spent the morning riding with my friend Tyler. When I rode into our drive, Dad was on a ladder. He was painting Mom's rose trellis. He had just built it the day before. He was painting it green.

I got off Joker by the pasture gate near the drive.

Dad called out to us. "Hi, Scott," he'd said. "Did you guys have a nice ride?"

"Sure did," I answered. "We rode across Tyler's pasture and over to the pond."

Tyler and I hadn't ridden very far. His mare was due to foal soon.

Then Dad spoke to Joker. "Hi, fella. How ya doing?"

He shouldn't have said anything to Joker. Joker got all excited. He always did when someone spoke to him.

He ran over to Dad and greeted him with a friendly nicker. When he nodded his head up and down, his head hit the ladder. The bucket of paint came down right on top of Joker's head. Dad went flying through the air. He landed on top of Mom's favorite rosebush. The one we'd bought her for Mother's Day.

What a mess!

Mom took Dad to the doctor. He came home with his ankle bandaged. And man, was he mad! I'm not sure about some of the words he used. Mom kept putting her hand over his mouth. They must have been pretty bad.

Dad was determined to sell Joker right then and there.

"That darned horse!" he mumbled through Mom's fingers. "I've had it with him. He's been nothing but trouble since the day he came."

I pleaded for all I was worth. "Please, please, please, Dad!" I begged. "You can't sell him. I'd just die."

Dad didn't budge.

"Maybe he'll get better," I said, fumbling for words—the right words. "After he's been here a little longer."

I turned to Mom for help. But she was nearly as mad as Dad.

And Wayne was no help at all. Actually he made things worse. He wouldn't quit laughing.

"Dad!" I was yelling now. "I'll do anything! Anything!"

I knew I wasn't making any sense. What the heck could I do?

At last, Dad gave in. "One more time," he said. "Just one more time. And that's final."

Mom spent the rest of the day picking rose thorns out of Dad. Wayne and I didn't watch, but we were pretty sure where most of them were.

It took over two weeks to get all the green paint off Joker. It took nearly that long for Dad's sprained ankle to heal.

And now, once again, Dad was mad.

"We can't keep a horse that acts the way he does, Scott," Dad said. "I've never heard of a horse that does such crazy things. I think that's why his owners sold him. They had to get rid of him."

"And that's why he was so cheap," Mom added. "A good horse should have cost twice that much. King cost a lot more."

Then Wayne started in. "Well, one thing's for sure," he said. "His name is perfect for him. What a Joker!"

I couldn't argue about that. I knew he was probably right.

The pony had already been named when we got him. Dad said we should keep his name. That way, we wouldn't confuse him.

"And he's confused enough as it is," my smart-mouthed brother said.

I hate calling my horse Joker. Sometimes I secretly call him Beauty, or Midnight, or Champion.

Sometimes, when I ride him at full gallop across the pasture, I'm Alexander the Great. And he's Bucephalus, the wonder horse of the world.

I ride swiftly into battle with my sword held tightly in my outstretched hand. "Charge, oh mighty mount!" I roar. "On to victory!"

Joker loves it. The louder I yell, the faster he goes. He holds his head high and lifts his tail in the wind.

It's our favorite game. We play it a lot.

But I've never told anyone about it. Not even my very best friend, Tyler Flemming.

Tyler's horse is a pretty little buckskin mare. Her name is Misty.

Tyler feels bad when Joker gets in trouble, the same as I do. He's given me lots of advice. But so far nothing has worked.

Dad pushed his chair back. He got up from the table. "I'm not kidding, Scott," he said. "The very next time Joker does something nutty, I'll put an ad in the paper and sell him. We can't keep a horse like that."

I swallowed hard to keep from sniffling.

"It can't be helped, honey," Mom said. "He's a real problem. We may as well own a goat."

"You never see King acting that way," Wayne gloated. "He's a perfect horse."

How right he was.

King was Wayne's beautiful sorrel. He had won all kinds of prizes and ribbons. He was a model of good conduct.

Everyone was always comparing Joker to King. That just made Joker look even worse.

But it didn't make me love him any less.

3

What a Horse!

My friend Tyler was really excited Monday morning. He jumped on the bus and flopped down next to me.

"Guess what, Scott!" Tyler exclaimed. "Misty had her foal last night! A filly. It looks just like Misty." He was all out of breath. "She's really pretty. I named her Dash."

"Cool," I answered.

I felt guilty. I'd been waiting for him. I wanted to talk to him. I needed someone to tell my troubles to. Someone who could understand how I felt. And Tyler was always a good listener. He always gave me the support I needed.

Now I hated to spoil his good news with my bad news.

"Gol—" I tried to sound cheerful. "That's neat, Tyler. I'll stop by after school and see her. Okay?"

"Sure," he answered. "You're going to love her."

Lucky Tyler. He had a nice, well-behaved horse. And now a foal of his very own. And no big brother with a smart mouth.

Tyler knows me pretty well. So well that he guessed something was wrong.

"You okay, Scott?" he asked.

So I told him all about the awful weekend.

"Oh, man," he groaned. "Not again."

I tried to swallow. I had a lump in my throat.

"Dad says he's—he's putting an ad in the paper," I said. "He's going to—to sell Joker." I had to swallow the lump again. "If he does one more thing." My voice was shaking. "And—and I'm pretty sure he will."

Tyler slugged me on the shoulder. "That's rough, Scott," he said. "But, well, maybe it won't happen."

Tyler was a special friend. He always felt the same as I did about everything. No matter what. Tyler and I had been friends since kindergarten.

The bus pulled up in front of school. Tyler and I were in the same class this year. We headed toward Miss Lee's room. Every Monday started the same. Miss Lee asked us to share a story with the class.

"About anything that has happened to you," she explained. "Or to someone you know."

She always said, "Try to make it interesting to the rest of the class."

Well, Joker's laundry stunt would be interesting. The class would love it. But no way was I telling it.

I'd already learned my lesson. Once, I told the class about one of Joker's antics. They danced around the whole day singing "Tiptoe Through the Tulips."

We were just sitting down to breakfast—Mom, Dad, Wayne, and me. All of a sudden, there was Joker in the window. Right over Mom's flower bed. He was nodding his head back and forth—with a tulip in his teeth.

Mom let out a scream. Wayne guffawed. Dad swore. I tried not to giggle, but I couldn't help it.

That is, until I followed Mom outside. We looked at her flower bed. And it wasn't so funny anymore.

That wasn't the only thing I got teased about. Stacy Robbins' father was a doctor. The doctor who treated Dad's sprained ankle. So the class knew about the paint incident.

I got pretty tired of kids calling Joker a dumb horse.

Miss Lee was standing in the front of the room. "I hope you have some interesting stories to share this morning," she said.

I didn't.

Miss Lee called on us alphabetically. With Yates as a last name, I had a little time to come up with something.

Bryce Adams was first. He told about buying baseball cards at the new card shop. As if anybody cared.

Kate Bowman's great-aunt Milly came to visit. All the way from London. Whoop-de-do.

Ron Davis bought a hamster. That was cool.

Some of the kids told about movies they'd seen. Most of them had seen the same one.

Then Tyler told about Misty's new foal. The kids asked a lot of questions. Some of them were kind of dumb.

"Did you watch it being born?" "How big is it?" "Is it her first baby?" "Is it your very own?" "When can you ride it?"

Miss Lee finally said, "Let's move on now."

Beth Garret shared a fishing story. She'd gone fishing with her father and caught a ten-inch trout. So she said.

I guess maybe I was a little jealous of Tyler. He was getting a lot of attention over Misty.

Tyler and I were the only kids in the class who had horses. And I didn't talk about mine anymore.

But right then I made up my mind I was going to talk about Joker. I was sick of everyone laughing at him. I'd make him a hero. I'd make him the greatest horse that ever lived!

At last, Alex Wells finished his dopey story about his piano recital.

I was ready. I crossed my fingers behind my back. Hard. I felt my knuckles crack. I took a deep breath.

"It was Saturday afternoon," I started. "I was riding my big black horse alongside the highway."

Bryce Adams snickered.

Miss Lee stared at him.

I was careful not to say Joker's name. That would made everyone laugh.

"I'd taught my horse to prance " I said. "To raise his knees up to his chest—just like show horses do."

Alex yawned. Loudly.

"My horse learned fast," I went on. "My brother wants me to teach his horse how to prance. But I'm not sure I can."

Stacy picked up a pencil and started doodling on her notebook.

I gritted my teeth, then continued. "He was stepping along with his head held high," I demonstrated.

The picture unfolded in my mind. The story got better and better.

"There was a lot of traffic. Drivers were slowing down. They were looking at us in amazement."

Bryce snickered again. So did some other kids.

"Then—ah—all of a sudden—uh—" Think fast, I told myself.

"A tiny child toddled onto the highway," I said. I drew in my breath. "I couldn't believe my eyes. A truck was coming fast. Too fast to stop in time."

I sucked in more air.

Then I sucked in more air.

"Then, my brave, fearless horse gave a screeching whinny. He dashed into the traffic and snatched up the child with his teeth. By his T-shirt!"

I paused. My mouth was so dry I had to swallow three times.

"Then my horse dropped the kid on the ground just off the highway. Just as the truck reached the very spot where the little kid had been."

My mind raced. Oh, yes—the parents.

"Suddenly, the child's parents came running toward us. They were so happy and grateful. They were surprised at how brave my horse was."

More snickers.

"The father tried to pay me. He tried to give me—uh—one hundred dollars," I said. "Of course, I couldn't take it. Jok—my horse had only done what his strong, brave heart had told him to do."

I figured that was a good place to stop. So I did.

I looked around the room. Bryce was shaking his head and rolling his eyes. Alex was yawning. Stacy was reading a book. Two kids had their heads on their desks.

"What a nice—story," Miss Lee said.

So what if no one believed me. It was the best story of all.

For a long time, I stood there feeling foolish.

Then, of all things, Tyler started clapping. I felt more foolish than ever. Leave it to Tyler to be on my side.

I stopped at Tyler's after school to see Misty's foal. Boy, was she ever cute. Stumbling around on her long, wobbly legs.

I stayed for almost an hour. Not once did Tyler say anything about my stupid story. Neither did I.

4

Tiptoeing in the Tulips

By Wednesday, things at home had cooled down a little. Nobody said much about Joker.

Until Wayne spoke up. "Mom, where's the mate to my blue sock?" he asked.

I held my breath. Some of the mates to my socks were missing too. They'd come up missing after Saturday.

Mom looked right at me. "I'll give you three guesses," she said.

"Huh!" Wayne snorted, looking dumb.

"Oh, yeah," he said when he caught on. "That crazy horse probably ate it."

I changed the subject fast—to baseball standings. Dad and I were really into baseball.

Mom made peanut butter waffles and crisp bacon. Cool! My favorite. I decided right then it was going to be a great day.

To top it off, I had new shoes. When I got to school, six kids said they liked them.

One of them was Erica Stanfield! The girl I had liked since last fall. She'd been new in the class.

Erica Stanfield was like no girl I'd ever liked. And I had liked a few.

In kindergarten and first grade, it was Angie Pope. She could make the best clay snakes. But she moved away.

In second grade, it was Katie Mills. Until she gave me a black eye—just for giving my tuna fish sandwich to Lisa Brown. Katie didn't even like tuna fish.

In third and fourth grades, I didn't like girls too much. I liked horses.

That was when Tyler got Misty. I spent all my time at his place. I helped him curry Misty. And we rode double. That was when Wayne got King too. But Wayne wouldn't let me around him. Once in a while, he'd let me ride double with him. But just around the pasture.

Next, I really liked Jessica Lowe. She was something else. She still was, but now she was a foot taller than me. Now Tyler liked her. He didn't care how tall she was. Jessica was the first girl he'd ever liked.

Erica Stanfield was really something too. Even more than Jessica. She had long blonde hair. Jessica's hair was brown and short.

Erica had never even looked at me until that morning. She was on her way to the pencil sharpener when suddenly she tripped over my foot. It was sticking out in the aisle.

"Gol!" I exclaimed. "I'm sorry."

She regained her balance. She looked down at my shoes. Then she looked straight into my eyes. "Cool shoes," she said.

My heart jumped right up into my throat. She liked me! She liked me!

Wonderful Wednesday!

So far, anyway. How could the day possibly get any better?

Wednesday was pizza day. I traded my salad to Kyle Martin for his serving. I couldn't believe that anyone in the world would like salad better than pizza. Especially salad with celery in it. Yuck! Kyle's whole family was into health food. Kyle ate some really weird stuff.

After lunch, Miss Lee started to hand back our graded history reports. She didn't look at all pleased. "I'm sorry to say that most of your reports are not acceptable," she said. "They will have to be done over."

I groaned along with the rest of the class.

"Some of these," Miss Lee said, "have been copied straight from the encyclopedia."

Not mine! Mom made sure I never copied word for word. I don't have to anyway. I have a way with words. Everyone says so.

I know words that Wayne doesn't know. And he's in high school.

Miss Lee went on. "Most of them have not been researched at all."

Mine had! I used three sources. The encyclopedia and two history books. Just the way Dad told me to.

Miss Lee had said to pick someone and do a 200-word report.

"It should be about someone who really interests you," she said. "Someone in history."

That had been the difficult part. I'd had a hard time deciding. Lots of historical people interested me.

First I'd picked Christopher Columbus. He interested me. I'd figured if he hadn't discovered America, I wouldn't even be here. But then I'd decided that if he hadn't, someone else would've.

Probably Thomas Edison. He discovered a lot of things. Or maybe he invented them.

I'd thought about doing Dr. Martin Luther King. But I'd found out that Tyler was doing him. I liked George Washington, John Paul Jones, and Daniel Boone.

I had almost decided on Paul Revere. Then I came across this picture in a history book. A picture of a handsome man on a beautiful black horse. A horse that looked like Joker.

It was General Ulysses S. Grant. He was a general in the Civil War. He later became the eighteenth president of the United States. He served two terms, so he must have been a good president.

He'd interested me a lot. So I did a 300-word report on him and his beautiful horse.

And now Miss Lee was saying that it was not acceptable?

But, how could she?

"However," Miss Lee was saying. "One student turned in a very interesting report." She was smiling now.

She motioned to me. "Scott Yates," she said. "Will you please read this out loud to the class?"

Needless to say, the class was impressed. So was I. It was even better than I'd thought. And I did a great job of reading it.

Miss Lee said my report was especially well-written.

My great day continued. I got a perfect grade in

spelling. In PE, we played baseball, and I hit a super home run.

I could hardly wait to get home and tell Mom about the history report, the spelling grade, and the home run. I wouldn't tell her about trading my salad for pizza. I didn't think she'd be interested in that.

I wouldn't tell her that I'd found out that Erica Stanfield liked me either. She'd tell Dad and Wayne. Dad might not tease me, but Wayne would. In his dumb way.

It was exactly 3:35 p.m. when my wonderful day ended. That's when I stepped off the bus in front of my house.

Mom was in the yard. She was standing beside the flower bed she'd been working on so hard. Or rather— what used to be a flower bed. Now it was only a mess of trampled plants.

Joker was sprinting back and forth in his pasture along the fence by the driveway. He was shaking his head and whinnying in snorts. He always did that when he got put back in the pasture—after he'd gotten loose.

The pasture gate was tied with a rope. The big metal clasp was lying on the ground.

Daffodils, tulips, and pansies were scattered all over. The ones that weren't smashed in the ground.

This was the third time.

Oh, Joker. I choked back tears as I walked toward Mom.

"Hi, Mom," I half whispered. "I—I'm awful—awful sorry."

"Sorry!" Mom snorted. "Hah! What good is sorry?"

Joker was bobbing his head up and down, happy to see me. I tried not to look at him.

Mom turned toward Joker. She was glaring. "Hah!" she snorted again.

She sounded almost like Joker when she snorted like that. So much that he answered with a snort of his own.

Mom threw a tulip at him—bulb and all. It fell short by a mile.

I could see King out in the pasture, calmly grazing. He was being a perfect model horse.

I began to plead with Mom. "Please don't tell Dad, Mom," I begged. "He'll put an ad in the paper and sell Joker."

"Right!" she answered. "That's exactly what he'll do. And it's about time."

"But, Mom! I'd just—just die without him," I moaned.

"Well, I won't!" Mom spat. She spread her hands out over the flower bed. "Look at that! Look!"

I looked. It was pretty bad. Some of Joker's tracks were almost a foot deep.

"But—but, Mom," I began. Quick! Think something, I told myself. "The—the cat does worse things than that in your flower bed. And you wouldn't sell her. Not for anything."

Mom threw her head back. She put her hands on her hips. "For your information, young man, Joker did that too. Only he didn't cover it up."

I looked again. Mom was right. Gol! It had wiped out at least six pansy plants. And did it ever smell!

I wanted to ask her if it wasn't good fertilizer. But I decided I'd better not.

I got the shovel out of the barn and cleaned it up. I was glad Wayne wasn't home. I could just hear him.

I helped Mom fix the flower bed. I didn't talk the whole time I was working. I just sniffed a lot and tried my best to look pitiful.

Oh, how I hoped it would work.

5

A Sticky Situation

Mom didn't say anything to me either—the whole time we were working. I gathered up all the tulips I could. And the daffodils. They were okay. But most of the pansies were destroyed. Mom and I replanted everything.

I wanted so bad to tell Mom about my history report. About the nice things Miss Lee had said about it. And about the perfect spelling grade and the terrific home run I'd hit.

But at the moment, it didn't seem like a good idea. Mom was stabbing the ground with her trowel and grunting with every stab. I took that to mean she was very angry. I guess I couldn't really blame her. If I didn't love Joker so much, I'd be mad at him too. Because he got me in so much trouble.

Right now, though, I wanted to concentrate on being sorry and pitiful.

When we finished the job, Mom stood up. She scraped the mud off her knees with her trowel. We were both pretty dirty.

"I'm going to take a shower," she said.

She didn't even notice how sad I was looking.

"I think I'll take Joker for a ride," I said. "To calm him down."

"A little late for that," Mom answered. "Besides, that horse doesn't calm down. Ever."

Now I felt worse than ever. I had to get away. To be alone with Joker.

I had an idea.

"Mom," I said. "Would you help me saddle Joker, please?"

"Why?" she asked. "You've never had to have help before."

"I—I have a—a blister on my finger," I said. "From all the digging I did."

It wasn't a fib. I really did have a tiny blister. I thought if Mom helped me, Joker might win her over just a little bit. She did like him. At least she always had before.

She helped me saddle him. Joker nuzzled her neck. Mom just glared at him. How could she resist him? I wondered. He was so lovable. He nuzzled her again. She pushed his nose away.

"Keep your nasty slobber to yourself," she said.

But I could see a smile—a very little smile.

I mounted my horse, and I started down the drive.

"Don't be gone too long," Mom called. "I want you here when your father gets home. Understand?"

"Yes, Mom," I said, swallowing hard.

I rode Joker down the gravel road to an old logging road. Then we went up to a wooded area. Flynn Butte was about a mile from home. It was a great place to ride.

My eyes were blurred as I rode along. It was so hard to keep from crying. I thought how awful it would be if they sold my pony. How could I live without him?

I reached forward and scratched Joker's ears. He nickered and bobbed his head up and down to let me know how much he liked it.

I thought of how much fun we'd had together. How neat it was the day I got him for my birthday. And what a surprise. The last thing I'd expected was a horse of my very own.

I was so sure I was going to get a TV for my room. That would have been good too. But compared to a horse! Of my very own! Nothing could be better than Joker.

Even Wayne was in on the big surprise.

My birthday had been on a Saturday. When I walked into the kitchen, Mom was putting breakfast on the table. She'd fixed French toast and ham. Dad stuck a lighted candle into my French toast. Then they all sang "Happy Birthday." I looked around, but I didn't see any packages.

After we ate, Wayne jumped up. "Hey, shrimp. Want to help me feed King?" he asked. "I'll take you for a run across the pasture."

"Sure," I answered.

I was a little surprised. But sometimes he did let me ride double with him. And it was my birthday. I guess he figured that was sort of a present.

I put on my jacket and baseball cap. Then I followed Wayne to the barn. Wayne kept King in the barn at night sometimes. Like when it was cold or rainy.

I could hear a nicker from inside.

"King must be eager to get out," I said.

"I guess so," Wayne answered.

He opened the barn door and there was Joker. He was bobbing his head up and down, nickering.

I was speechless. "Is—is it mine?" I gasped.

Wayne said, "Happy Birthday, shrimp."

The first thing Joker did was pull my cap off with his teeth.

Wayne guffawed.

Suddenly, Mom and Dad were standing in the doorway. "Meet Joker, Scott," said Dad.

Mom really laughed when she saw Joker waving my cap back and forth in his teeth.

It was the greatest feeling! The greatest feeling in the world! A horse of my very own!

Joker nickered when I stopped scratching his ears.

"You're spoiled," I laughed.

Joker shook his head.

"Gol, Joker," I said. "I wish you wouldn't get in so much trouble. Why can't you be like King?"

Joker flicked his ears.

"I wouldn't want you to be just like King," I explained. I didn't want to hurt his feelings. "I love you more than I could ever love King—or any other horse."

We came to the log bridge. It spanned a gulf that ran through the valley below. Across the bridge was a good riding trail. Tyler and I had ridden it a lot. Wayne and his friends went there to hunt for agates. They were into rock collecting. Tyler and I collected some too.

But today, I didn't want to ride the trail. So I dismounted and flopped down on the soft, cool grass.

My pony grazed. He was so contented. He didn't have the slightest idea he'd done anything wrong. He never did.

It was terrible having people hate and laugh at your pet. A pet you loved more than anything in the world.

How could I stand to lose him? The last six months had been so wonderful. Except when he was in trouble, of course. And that was a lot.

But I loved him so much. I couldn't hold it back any longer. I rolled over on my stomach and cried until I couldn't cry anymore.

A loud nicker from Joker made me sit up. I looked around. My pony was walking very slowly toward the bridge. His head was down and his ears were flattened.

"What is it, Joker?" I called. "What do you see?"

I stood up and rubbed my eyes with my fists.

As I moved closer, I saw what Joker was looking at. A big, fat porcupine. It was sitting on the bridge, chewing on a limb.

Oh, no, I thought. I panicked. "You'd better stay back!" I yelled. "If you know what's good for you!"

Joker edged closer. Hearing my voice only made him braver.

"No, Joker! No!" I yelled. "Get back!"

It was no use. Joker wouldn't obey me. I ran to him, but I was too late. Joker let out a scream of pain. And he reared high into the air.

"Joker! Joker!" I cried.

Joker galloped off through the woods, still neighing wildly. I thought he must have been out of his mind with pain and fear.

I finally found him standing in a thicket. He was whimpering and trembling all over. His coat was covered with foamy lather. There were four quills in his nose.

"Poor boy," I soothed. I patted Joker's neck. "Come on, Joker. I'll take you home."

I felt sorry for him.

I led him out of the woods and started home. I could hardly see where I was going, my eyes were so full of tears. I walked as fast as I could. Joker trembled all the way.

Luckily, I got him into the barn without being seen. I got Dad's pliers and pulled out the quills. Joker didn't move a muscle. He seemed almost in shock from the awful thing that had happened to him. I put salve on his swollen nose. Then I took off his saddle and rubbed him down. When I gave him a big kiss—right on his nose—he just stood dead still.

Moments later, I walked into the kitchen.

"It's about time," Wayne said. "I was just going to look for you."

I must have gasped. "Why?" I asked at last.

"Mom said to," Wayne answered. "She was afraid something might have happened to you." Wayne laughed his dumb laugh. He smacked me on the back.

"After all, you were on that kooky horse of yours."

"Very funny!" I snapped.

I sucked in my breath. I hoped I didn't look different. Oh, please, please, I prayed. Don't let anyone ever find out about the porcupine.

We were almost finished with dinner before I realized something. Mom hadn't said a word about the flower bed. I studied her face, but it didn't tell me anything.

Gol, was it possible that my pitiful act had worked? I thought so.

Just before I dozed off that night, she tiptoed into my room. She kissed me on the cheek. She didn't know I was awake. I made a little sobbing sound. She kissed me again.

6

Not Your Average Horse

It took about three days for the swelling on Joker's nose to go down. No one had noticed it. But they noticed something else.

Joker was different. He was quieter and calmer—not like himself at all.

"I wonder if we should have the vet look at him," Dad suggested. "There may be something wrong."

Dad was serious.

"I—I think he's okay," I stammered. "He's just—just getting more used to being here."

"After six months?" Wayne said. "Are you kidding?"

Wayne didn't believe Joker had changed. "He's just plotting something," Wayne said. "That horse will never change."

"Let's not give up hope," said Mom.

Gol, was she on Joker's side?

But then she said, "Though I'm not sure there is any hope for him. He's not your average horse, after all."

"Well—well—who wants an average horse?" I asked. But I wished right away I hadn't said that.

"We do!" Mom, Dad, and Wayne exclaimed.

For over a week, nothing happened. Joker was behaving almost as well as King.

I reminded everyone of it every day. Mom and Dad were really pleased. So was I.

But Wayne said, "Just wait. He'll do something. You know how dumb he is."

"Joker is not dumb," I insisted. "He's just—just high-spirited. And a little curious at times."

"And dumb," Wayne retorted. "You don't see King doing the things Joker does."

"That's because King has no personality," I blurted. "He's dull—with a capital D."

What the heck made me say that?

But then I thought maybe I was right. Maybe that was the difference. King had no personality and Joker did. King might be a big, prize-winning, well-behaved horse. But he was dull. And no one could say that Joker was dull.

One day, Mom was baking apple pies. She discovered she was out of cinnamon. "I don't want to stop now and go to the store," she said. She was peeling apples. "Would one of you go for me?"

There was a little store not far away.

"I'll go," Wayne offered. "I'll ride King."

"I'll go too," I said. "I'll ride Joker."

"No way!" exclaimed Wayne. "I'll go by myself. I'm not going to be embarrassed by that stupid horse."

He went on and on until Mom told him to knock it off. "Both of you go," she said.

We were riding down the road when we heard a motorcycle coming. And it was coming fast. I tensed a little. Traffic made Joker nervous. Especially something as loud as a motorcycle.

"Hold him firm, Scott," Wayne said. "Raise his head—like this. And talk to him. Keep talking to him."

I watched Wayne hold the reins close to King's neck. King raised his head—just a little.

Then I tried it. I held the reins against Joker's neck the way Wayne did. "Steady, boy," I said. "Steady now."

I kept talking to him gently as the motorcycle raced past. Joker didn't even flinch. That had never happened before.

"Not bad," Wayne grinned at me. "For a horse who is—uh—high-spirited."

That was something coming from Wayne. It was close to a compliment.

But the very next day, Wayne was making fun of Joker the same as always.

Joker was chasing a raven around the pasture. It was one of his favorite pastimes. The raven would cry, "Caw! Caw!" And Joker would whinny.

Sometimes Joker would chase the ravens until he wore himself out. Dad said he thought the ravens enjoyed it as much as Joker did.

"Get a load of that dumb nag!" Wayne roared. "What a nerd!"

I didn't mind him laughing. I thought it was really funny too. But I hated it when he called Joker a dumb nag.

I spent a lot of time at Tyler's, seeing the new foal. She was so cute. She had long skinny legs and a head that looked too big for the rest of her.

"I can't believe how fast she's growing," Tyler said.

I told him how well Joker was behaving. "He hasn't been in trouble for ages," I said. "Even Wayne said something good about him."

Tyler was as happy and proud as I was.

I had finally told Tyler about the porcupine. He'd promised not to tell anyone.

"I don't want anyone making fun of him either," he'd said. "Don't worry, Scott. You can depend on me."

I knew that. I'd counted on Tyler since we were five years old. I told him all my secrets. I couldn't count all the times he'd covered for me.

But I could count the times I'd covered for him. Zero. I couldn't remember Tyler ever doing much of anything wrong. Tyler was just about perfect.

In the back of my mind, I giggled. Like King, I thought. Perfect. But he was still my best friend.

I rode over to Tyler's one day to see Dash—the new foal.

"It's really weird," I told Tyler. "But since that porcupine slapped Joker, he's been acting so much different. So well behaved."

I took Joker's saddle off so he could run around the pasture.

Tyler got two sodas from his mother. We climbed on the top rail of the corral and watched the horses. Joker and Misty always got along fine. But she was a little nervous since foaling. She even nipped toward Joker. He must have thought she was playing. He ran around in circles kicking up his hind legs.

Tyler laughed. "I don't know, Scott," he said. "He acts the same as always to me."

"But he is different," I insisted. "A lot. He hasn't broken out for a long time. And you know how he hates being in that pasture."

"I guess it could be because of the porcupine," Tyler said. "Maybe it did calm him down a little."

I hoped so. But if it was that, it had been a hard lesson.

Joker was crazy about the foal. He followed it around, sniffing at it. Misty nickered a gentle warning now and then. After a while she seemed to understand that Joker wouldn't harm her baby. So she relaxed.

When it was time to go, Joker came right to me. Usually he made a game of it. Bobbing his head up and down. Stepping to one side as I was about to catch him.

Wayne had told me it was my own fault for letting him get away with it. But I didn't know how to make him stop.

On the way home from Tyler's, a noisy sports car sped by. I held Joker's reins the way Wayne had shown me. And I talked to him. "It's all right, Joker. It's all right."

Joker paid no attention to the car.

Tyler started riding Misty again. We rode together in her pasture. Dash would follow along behind. I thought Joker might act up, but he didn't. He did nicker a little at the foal, like he was saying, "Come on, slowpoke."

Joker always came to me when I called him now. No more games of tag.

"Oh, Joker I'm so proud of you," I told him. He pushed his cold nose against my neck. "And I love you so much."

I was sure that everything was going to be all right from now on.

But Wayne wasn't.

"Okay," Wayne said. "So he's acting a little better lately. I wouldn't count on it to last." He smirked. "After all, he's got a name to live up to."

I didn't care what my brother thought. I knew that Joker had given up his bad habits.

Everything would be fine. Joker was mine for keeps.

7

Out of Chances

I was so excited over the way things were turning out. Joker had finally settled down. He was being the kind of horse people couldn't make fun of.

Well—most of the time. He still did things that some people might think were a little weird.

There was a small birch tree in the pasture that Joker used for a rump-scratching post.

"We should put a grass skirt on him," Dad said. "He looks like he's doing the hula."

The problem was the tree was so small it always bent. So Joker always ended up sitting on the ground with a surprised look on his face.

That always cracked up Dad and Wayne.

One time, Dad brought some of his friends home to watch it. It was really embarrassing. They said rude things about Joker.

"That horse must have been brain damaged at birth," said one.

"Is that what you call horse sense?" laughed another.

Very funny.

Wayne declared, "If it was any other horse but Joker, he would have figured it out by now."

"Maybe he does it on purpose," I suggested. "Because he knows it makes people laugh."

"Yeah, sure," said Wayne.

Joker loved apples. He did something that some people, like Mom, thought was gross. He'd chew up the apple, swallow, then blow out his lips. Apple juice, bits of peelings, and seeds would fly out. Right in the face of whoever had given him the apple.

That cracked my brother up too. Until he was the one who got it in the face.

But these things were just part of Joker's neat personality. They weren't things that caused trouble.

No more kicking down the gate. No more destroying things. No more running away.

Ever since I'd gotten Joker, he'd tried to be friends with King. But King would have nothing to do with him.

"It's because Joker is not as good as King," Wayne tried to tell me. "King won't have anything to do with a horse who isn't his equal."

"It's because he's stuck-up," I replied. "Just like you."

My brother laughed in my face. "Whoever heard of a stuck-up horse?" he asked. "He's simply smart enough to realize that your pony isn't bright. He wants nothing to do with him."

At times, King actually had been mean to Joker. And all Joker wanted was to be friends. Twice King had kicked Joker. And once he'd bitten him bad enough that it bled.

So I was really surprised when, one morning, I saw King rubbing his long nose against Joker's neck.

For a moment, I thought he was going to bite my pony again. Then I realized he was being friendly. When Joker nickered softly, King answered. Just like he was saying, "Let's be friends."

Wayne's school bus left before mine, so he didn't see it. But just wait till he finds out, I thought. He'll eat his words.

I could barely wait to tell Tyler. Not just about that,

but about how well Joker was behaving. How smoothly things were going at home.

Tyler was as pleased as I was. "Hey, Scott, that's great," he said. "You don't have to worry anymore about your parents selling him."

It looked like the start of another great day. I hoped this one would last longer than the last one had.

Miss Lee chose a really good book for read-aloud time. Oh, sweet bliss! It was a horse story. About a wild stallion named Whitey. I loved it, and so did the rest of the class.

I got a B+ on a social studies test—my most hated subject.

And the best part of the whole day was—Erica ate lunch with me!

Tyler and Jessica sat with us. But I only had eyes for Erica. Ever since the day she'd finally noticed me, she'd gotten prettier and prettier. If that was possible.

She and Tyler had been the only kids in the class who hadn't sneered or laughed at my story. The one about Joker saving the little kid. Even Jessica had snickered a little.

It was plain to see that Jessica had gotten over me. It was Tyler all the way now. But that was okay.

After school, Wayne's smart mouth was the same as always. He explained why King was making friends with Joker. "He feels sorry for your pony," Wayne said. "He knows how terrible it must be to be so dumb."

Then he said something really rotten. "After all, sometimes I even treat you nice—out of pity."

"You couldn't be nice if you tried," I snapped.

Wayne was ready with a smart reply, but Mom stepped in. "One more word out of either of you, and you'll go without TV for a week. Maybe a month."

She didn't sound like she meant it though. Seconds later, she poured two glasses of milk for us. And she put a plate of cookies, warm from the oven, on the table.

Chocolate chip!

My mom made the best cookies. And pies, and cakes, and pizzas!

I was on my fifth cookie when a loud neigh and a crashing sound almost made me spill my milk.

"It's Joker!" Wayne shouted. "It's got to be!"

We all ran into the yard. Wayne was right. The gate was hanging by one hinge. And Joker was tearing across the lawn toward the road.

A big farm truck, filled with sheep, was going by the house.

Wayne scratched his head. "What's that crazy horse doing?"

"Joker! Joker!" I shouted. "Come back here!" I even whistled as hard as I could.

But he was chasing the truckload of sheep, neighing with every breath he took. I'd never seen him run like that.

I could have died. I'd been so sure that Joker had changed. That he was mine for keeps. I knew now that this was the end of everything. Mom and Dad wouldn't give him another chance. And I guess I couldn't really blame them. All I could do was stand there being miserable.

Until Wayne jerked my arm. "Come on," he ordered. "Get your bike. We have to catch that fool horse before he really gets into trouble."

I never pedaled so fast in my life. But as fast as I was going, Wayne was way ahead of me.

"Hurry up, Scott," he kept shouting.

"I—I—am," I panted. My chest hurt. My eyes were burning. I had a pain in my side.

I could still see the truck ahead with my pony close behind. I didn't think the truck driver knew he was being chased by a horse. But it sounded as though the sheep did. I could hear the bleating from as far back as I was.

When we reached town, we caught up with the truck at a red light. We yelled at the top of our lungs at Joker. He wouldn't pay any attention.

Joker reared high in the air. He pawed at the back of the truck. The poor sheep were nearly trampling one another to death.

Suddenly, there was the truck driver, yelling his bald head off. "What's going on?" he shouted. "Get that harebrained horse out of here." He used some pretty strong language.

Then a policeman came.

What a commotion!

Hundreds of bleating sheep. A whinnying horse. And at least two dozen people lined up on the sidewalk—laughing themselves sick.

A man brought us a rope. While the policeman wrote stuff down in his book, the man tied the rope around Joker's neck.

Wayne rode off and left me behind. I had to pedal home, leading my horse by the rope. All by myself. Joker was so tired he kept stopping. "Come on, Joker," I begged. I was hoarse from yelling so much.

It was the most embarrassing thing that had ever happened to me in my whole life.

Dinner that night was a disaster. I felt so rotten. I could hardly see my plate. And I could hardly swallow. I think it was liver and lima beans, which I hate anyway.

My head ached from Mom and Dad hollering.

"I knew we should have gotten rid of that horse the first time he got out and trampled my flower bed," Mom said.

I didn't know anyone could chew as fast as Mom was chewing and talk at the same time.

The policeman had been there when Dad got home from work. He gave Dad a ticket. "For allowing an animal to run at large," the policeman explained.

"I don't allow this animal to run at large!" Dad had shouted. "I absolutely forbid him to run at large!"

The policeman had grinned and walked away.

"I hope you understand, Scott," Dad said, his face bright red. "This fine is coming out of your allowance."

I didn't care about my allowance. I didn't care about anything. I could just die, I felt so awful.

Wayne wasn't saying anything. He was hunched over the table stirring the food around his plate.

It was probably my imagination, but he looked like he felt awful too.

Right after the policeman left, Dad called the newspaper office and placed a for-sale ad.

8

Joker or Hero?

The next morning, I walked downstairs to breakfast. The newspaper was lying on the kitchen table.

There was a picture of Joker on the front page. He was pawing at the truck. The caption read HORSE MAKES EWE-TURN ON MAIN STREET.

I didn't turn to the page with the for-sale ad. I couldn't stand to see it.

McLean County Unit #5
202-Chiddix

I don't remember ever having such a terrible day.

Bryce Adams followed me around all day. He kept saying, "Baa! Baa!"

The whole class was in hysterics. Except Tyler and Erica. They felt as bad as I did.

I think even Miss Lee was trying to keep from laughing. Although she kept telling the class it wasn't nice.

And it started raining that morning right after school started. It really poured all day. We couldn't go out for recess. I found a quiet corner in the library and pretended to read a book.

When I got off the school bus that afternoon, the roads were full of deep puddles. I didn't even glance toward the pasture when I heard Joker nickering a greeting. I couldn't stand to look at him. Especially knowing that in a short time he'd be gone.

No matter what he'd done, I still loved him more than anything in the world. I'd be so lost without him.

Mom had pretzels and orange juice for my snack. Any other time that was one of my favorite snacks. I liked to dip the pretzels in the orange juice. But not today.

I wondered if anyone had called about the ad. But I didn't want to ask.

"I know how bad you feel, honey," Mom said. "But you've got to understand. Sooner or later, Joker could cause serious trouble." She sighed. "He's already cost us a lot of money. Putting in new plants twice. Dad's doctor bill for his sprained ankle. And now a fifty-dollar ticket."

Then she added something I wished everyone had forgotten. "And what about the money we had to pay to have the car repaired?"

I hate to tell this, it's so awful. Joker actually attacked the car. Dad had just finished polishing it. It was really shiny. I think Joker saw his reflection in the fender. First he nickered at it. Then he slobbered all over it.

"Hey, knock it off!" Dad had thundered.

But it was too late. Joker reared in the air and came down on the fender with his front feet. It was a mess. I'm not sure why he did it. But I'm sure he had a good reason. A good reason for a horse anyway.

Mom went on. "We've spent so much money for the damage Joker has done. More than what we paid for him to begin with."

I didn't say anything. There wasn't anything to say. It was all true.

"Maybe someday we'll get you another horse," Mom said.

"I don't want another horse!" I cried. "I don't ever want another horse!"

Then Wayne came home from school in a bad mood. "Stupid rain," he grumbled. "If this keeps up, the Saturday trip will be ruined."

"What trip?" I asked.

"Matt Sills, Rob Jones, Tony Martinez, and I planned to go on a ride," Wayne answered. "We're riding up the old logging road to Flynn Butte. We're going to hunt for rocks.

"Matt found a neat carnelian there last week," Wayne continued. "Up the trail on the other side of the bridge where we find the agates."

It sounded like fun. I guess I envied Wayne and his friends. They all had well-behaved horses. Horses that never got in trouble.

Without thinking, I sighed. "I wish I could go with you," I mumbled.

"Are you kidding?" Wayne blurted. "No way can that stu—that horse go with us."

Wayne had been a little nicer since Joker's recent adventure with the sheep truck. Almost as though he felt bad for me. He'd even stopped saying mean things about my horse.

I couldn't help thinking about Wayne's trip. And how nice it would be to have one last day with Joker.

"Please, Wayne," I begged. "It—it'll be the last time."

Wayne looked like he was in agony. "Aw, Scott. You know how he is. He'll be a nuisance. And—and the guys will be there."

Wayne took a deep breath. Then just like that, he stopped being sorry. "That dumb horse isn't going. And that's final. So let it drop."

I did.

There was no school Friday because of the rain. The roads were so bad that the buses couldn't get through.

Wayne and I moped around all day. Wayne because he figured his trip was off. And me because of knowing I was losing Joker.

"If you want me to, Scott, I'll feed Joker until—" he offered.

He didn't finish. But I knew what he meant.

"Thanks," I whispered.

Saturday morning we woke to a beautiful sunny day. Wayne was in a wonderful mood. He even sang at the breakfast table while Mom packed his lunch for the trip.

I wanted so much to go I decided to swallow my pride and give it one more try. I begged and pleaded for all I was worth.

Then Mom joined in. "It would be a nice thing to do, Wayne," she said. "And it'll be Scott's last time with Joker."

Wayne finally gave in. "But I'm warning you," he said as he shook his finger right in my face. "If that crazy horse causes any trouble—"

Wayne's friends had a lot of fun teasing me about Joker. But I wasn't going to let it bother me. I was going to enjoy this last day with my pony in spite of their teasing.

Joker stepped along nicely as I rode along behind Wayne and the other boys. A couple of times he shook his head in protest against the tightly held reins. But he was behaving pretty well.

It was beautiful in the woods. And it smelled good from the rain. Some places on the trail were soft and muddy. So we had to detour around them. When we got close to the bridge, it was really muddy.

"We better go pretty slow up the trail," said Rob. "It's awful steep. And as soft as the ground is, the horses could slip and fall."

"Why don't we just stop at the bridge?" suggested Tony.

"Because the best agates are up on the flat," said Wayne. "That's where we found them before. By the waterfall."

"Yeah, right," Tony replied. "We'll just ride slow."

"Come on," said Wayne, taking the lead.

Joker started to follow. Then suddenly, with no warning, he bucked. He threw me off. And I landed on the ground with a thud.

With an ear-splitting whinny, Joker began running around and around in circles. He kicked his hind legs like mad.

The boys struggled to control their horses. Tony's horse bucked him off. So the other boys dismounted.

Wayne was furious. "That crazy horse of yours has gone loco!" he yelled. "I knew we shouldn't have let him come."

I lay on the ground staring in wonder. What was wrong with Joker? He'd never bucked me off before. Sure, he'd done a lot of strange things. But he was acting as though he'd lost his mind completely.

He was bucking wildly, and his whinnies were deafening. He had a wild look in his eyes. I'd never seen him look like that. Except the time—

All at once it hit me! I knew what was wrong with my pony. The porcupine! He was remembering the awful thing that had happened to him on the bridge. And he was terrified.

I jumped to my feet and ran to him. "Steady, Joker, steady," I soothed. I grabbed his reins. At last I was able to calm him. "It's all right, boy," I said. "It's all right."

"Oh, sure, it's all right!" Wayne howled. "It's fine to go off your rocker. For no reason at all. Even if it endangers lives."

The boys were all glaring at me. And at Joker.

I just stood there and said nothing. I couldn't let them know. I couldn't let them laugh at Joker anymore. I'd rather have them mad at him than making fun of him.

I fumbled for some excuse—some reason—for his actions. "Maybe—maybe something was hurting him," I said. "Maybe he had a pain—"

"He is a pain," grumbled Matt.

Wayne looked at me. He was really mad. "You take that stupid horse home!" he snapped. "I should've known better than to give in and let you bring him."

All the boys mounted their horses.

They started again on the road toward the bridge. But all of a sudden, Wayne's friend, Rob, pulled his horse to a stop. So hard that the horse reared a little.

"What's wrong?" asked Matt.

"I'm not sure," Rob said. He got off his horse. He knelt down on one knee. "Hey, you guys!" he hollered. "Holy cow! Come here!"

The other boys moved closer.

"Look here!" said Rob. "The heavy rain has washed the ground away from those timbers. Look!"

"I think you're right," Wayne gasped. "That bridge is ready to cave in."

Matt and Tony picked up a small log lying close by. With all their might, they threw it on the bridge.

In horror, we watched as the old timbers broke loose from the ground. Seconds later, they crashed at the bottom of the gulch.

"Wow!" they all exclaimed together.

Wayne turned toward me. His face was dead white. His eyes looked like they were about to pop out.

"How—how—" Wayne stammered. "How could Joker have known?"

"But he must have known," said Rob. "That's why he was acting so strangely."

"Man!" cried Matt. "He was warning us not to go on the bridge."

Wayne walked over to where I was standing with my mouth hanging open.

"Scott," Wayne said, "I take back everything I ever said about that dumb—uh—that wonderful horse."

"That goes for me too," Matt said. "If it hadn't been for him, we'd all be at the bottom of that gulch."

"Joker saved our lives," Tony said. "What a horse!"

"Wait till we tell Mom and Dad," said Wayne. He gave me a big hug. "No way will they ever sell Joker."

I think I was in shock. I couldn't believe what I was hearing. They actually thought Joker was a hero.

Oh, sweet bliss! For the first time, Joker was being praised instead of made fun of.

I had a terrible time trying to keep a straight face. What if Wayne and his friends knew the real reason for Joker's behavior? I thought. What a laugh they would have. I would never live it down. Never.

But they'd never laugh at Joker again now. He was a hero—even if it was by accident.

And another thing. I decided to change his name. Let's see—maybe Rex. Or Gallant. Or Dandy.

Or maybe—maybe I'd name him Hero.